# The Wizard of Oz

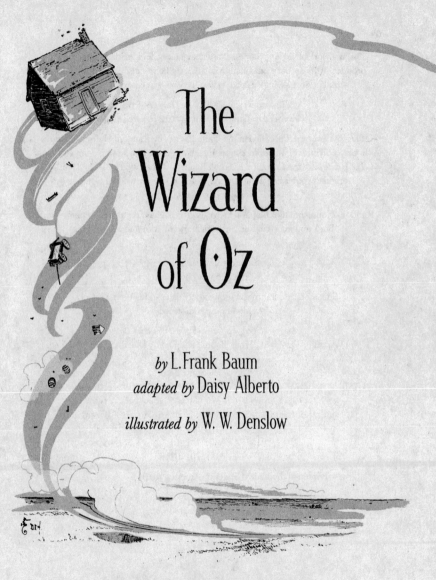

# The Wizard of Oz

*by* L. Frank Baum

*adapted by* Daisy Alberto

*illustrated by* W. W. Denslow

A STEPPING STONE BOOK™
Random House New York

Text copyright © 2012 by Daisy Alberto
Cover illustration copyright © 2012 by Greg Call

All rights reserved. Published in the United States by Random House Children's Books, a division of Random House, Inc., New York. This work is adapted from *The Wonderful Wizard of Oz* by L. Frank Baum and illustrated by W. W. Denslow, originally published in the United States by George M. Hill Company, Chicago, in 1900.

Random House and the colophon are registered trademarks and A Stepping Stone Book and the colophon are trademarks of Random House, Inc.

Visit us on the Web!
SteppingStonesBooks.com
randomhouse.com/kids

Educators and librarians, for a variety of teaching tools, visit us at
randomhouse.com/teachers

*Library of Congress Cataloging-in-Publication Data*
The Wizard of Oz / by L. Frank Baum ; adapted by Daisy Alberto. — 1st ed.
p. cm.
"A Stepping Stone book."
ISBN 978-0-375-86994-5 (trade) — ISBN 978-0-375-96994-2 (lib. bdg.) —
ISBN 978-0-375-98634-5 (ebook)
[1. Fantasy.]  I. Baum, L. Frank (Lyman Frank), 1856–1919. Wizard of Oz.
II. Title.
PZ7.A3217Wi 2012
[Fic]—dc23   2011021801

Printed in the United States of America  10 9

Random House Children's Books supports the First Amendment
and celebrates the right to read.

# CONTENTS

# CONTENTS

## CHAPTER ONE

# The Cyclone

Dorothy lived in Kansas with her uncle Henry and aunt Em. Their house stood in the middle of the great gray prairie. The house had been painted once, but the paint had faded. Now it was gray, too. Even Aunt Em and Uncle Henry were gray.

Toto was not gray. He was a little black dog. It was Toto who made Dorothy laugh and saved her from growing as gray as everything around her. He had black eyes that twinkled merrily. Toto played all day long, and Dorothy loved him dearly.

Today, however, Toto and Dorothy were not

playing. Uncle Henry sat on the doorstep. He looked at the sky. It was even grayer than usual.

Dorothy stood in the doorway with Toto. She looked at the sky, too.

The wind wailed. Suddenly, Uncle Henry stood up.

"There's a cyclone coming, Em!" he called. He ran toward the sheds where the cows and horses were kept.

Aunt Em dropped what she was doing. "Quick, Dorothy!" she screamed. "Run for the cellar!"

Aunt Em threw open the trapdoor in the floor of the house. She climbed down the ladder.

Dorothy caught Toto, who had jumped out of her arms. She started for the trapdoor.

The wind shrieked! The house shook!

Then a strange thing happened.

The house whirled around. It rose through the air! Dorothy felt as if she were going up in a

balloon. The wind lifted the house higher and higher.

Toto did not like it at all! He ran about the room, barking. When he got too near the open trapdoor, Dorothy dragged him away.

Dorothy wondered if she would be smashed to pieces. She crawled into her bed. Toto lay down beside her. Dorothy closed her eyes and fell fast asleep in the whirling house.

CHAPTER TWO

# The Munchkins

When Dorothy woke, the house was not moving. She ran and opened the front door.

There were patches of green grass and bright flowers all about! Birds sang in the bushes. A group of people was coming toward her. Three were men and one was an old woman. They were not as big as the grown-ups she was used to. In fact, they were about as tall as Dorothy herself.

The men were dressed in blue. The woman was wearing a white gown. It was sprinkled with little stars that glittered like diamonds. She walked up to Dorothy and bowed. "Welcome, most noble

Sorceress, to the Land of the Munchkins," she said. "We are so grateful to you for having killed the Wicked Witch of the East."

"There must be some mistake," Dorothy said. "I have not killed anything."

"But your house did," replied the woman.

Dorothy looked. Two feet with silver shoes on them were sticking out from under the house!

"Oh, dear!" cried Dorothy. "The house must have fallen on her! Who was she?"

"The Wicked Witch of the East, as I said," the woman answered. "She has held the Munchkins in slavery for years. Now they are free."

"Are *you* a Munchkin?" asked Dorothy.

"No. I am their friend. I am the Witch of the North."

"Gracious!" cried Dorothy. "Are you a real witch?"

"Yes," answered the little woman. "But I am a good witch."

"I thought all witches were wicked," said Dorothy.

"Oh, no," said the Good Witch. "There were four witches in the Land of Oz. Two of them, those who live in the North and the South, are good witches. Those who lived in the East and the West were, indeed, wicked witches. But now that you have killed one of them, there is but one Wicked Witch in the Land of Oz. The one who lives in the West."

"But," said Dorothy, "Aunt Em told me that the witches were all dead."

"In the civilized countries, I believe there are no witches left," said the Good Witch. "But the Land of Oz has never been civilized."

Just then the Munchkins all pointed to the bottom of the house.

The feet had disappeared. Nothing was left but the silver shoes.

"That is the end of her," explained the Witch of the North. "The shoes are yours." She picked up the silver shoes and handed them to Dorothy.

Dorothy carried the shoes into the house. Then she came out again and said, "I am anxious to get back to my aunt and uncle. Can you help me find my way?"

The Munchkins and the Witch shook their heads.

"A great desert surrounds this Land of Oz," explained the Good Witch. "None can cross it."

She balanced her cap on the end of her nose. "You could go to the City of Emeralds," said the Good Witch. "Perhaps Oz, the Great Wizard, will help you."

"Where is this city?" asked Dorothy.

"It is in the center of the Land of Oz," said

the Good Witch. "It is ruled by the Wizard."

"Won't you go with me?" pleaded Dorothy.

"No, I cannot," replied the Good Witch. "But I will give you my kiss. And no one will dare hurt a person who has been kissed by the Witch of the North." With that, she kissed Dorothy on the forehead. Her lips left a shining mark.

"The road to the City of Emeralds is paved with yellow brick," said the Witch. "You cannot miss it. Good-bye, my dear."

The three Munchkins bowed low and walked away. The Witch gave Dorothy a friendly nod. Then she whirled around three times and disappeared.

Toto was surprised. But Dorothy, knowing her to be a witch, was not surprised in the least.

## CHAPTER THREE

# How Dorothy Saved the Scarecrow

Dorothy went back into the house to get ready for her journey.

She had only one other dress. It was made of gingham, with white and blue checks. She changed into it, then took a basket and filled it with bread from the cupboard.

Dorothy spotted the silver shoes that had belonged to the Witch of the East. She took off her old shoes and tried on the silver ones. They fit as if they had been made for her.

Dorothy put the basket over her arm. "Come

along, Toto," she said. "We will go to the Emerald City and ask the Great Oz how to get back to Kansas!"

It did not take her long to find the road paved with yellow bricks that led toward the Emerald City.

As she and Toto walked along, Dorothy was surprised to see how pretty the country was. There were neat fences at the sides of the road, painted blue. Beyond them were fields of grain.

When they had gone several miles, Dorothy climbed to the top of a fence to rest. In the field beside the fence was a scarecrow.

"Good day," said the Scarecrow.

"Did you speak?" Dorothy asked in wonder.

"Certainly," answered the Scarecrow. "How do you do?"

"I'm pretty well, thank you," replied Dorothy politely. "How do *you* do?"

"I'm not feeling well," said the Scarecrow. "It is very tiresome being perched up here night and day."

"Can't you get down?" asked Dorothy.

"No. This pole is stuck up my back," said the Scarecrow. "If you will please take away the pole, I shall be greatly obliged."

Dorothy walked into the field. She lifted the Scarecrow off the pole. Since he was stuffed with straw, he was quite light.

"Thank you," said the Scarecrow. "Who are you? And where are you going?"

"My name is Dorothy," she said. "I am going to the Emerald City, to ask the Great Oz to send me back to Kansas."

"Where is the Emerald City?" he asked. "And who is Oz?"

"Don't you know?" Dorothy said in surprise.

"No. I don't know anything," the Scarecrow

answered sadly. "I am stuffed, so I have no brains."

"Oh," said Dorothy, "I'm awfully sorry."

"Do you think," the Scarecrow asked, "that if I go with you, Oz would give me some brains?"

"I cannot tell," Dorothy said. "But I'll ask Oz to do all he can for you."

"Thank you," answered the Scarecrow gratefully.

The Scarecrow and Dorothy walked back to the road. Dorothy helped the Scarecrow over the fence. Then they started along the yellow brick road together with Toto.

At noon they sat down by the roadside. Dorothy opened her basket. She offered a piece of bread to the Scarecrow, but he shook his head.

"I am never hungry," he said. "And it is lucky I am not, for my mouth is only painted on."

When Dorothy had finished her lunch, the

Scarecrow said, "Tell me something about the country you came from."

So Dorothy told him all about Kansas. She told him how gray everything was, and how the cyclone had carried her to this strange land.

The Scarecrow listened carefully. "I cannot understand why you should wish to go back to the gray place you call Kansas."

"That is because you have no brains," Dorothy answered. "No matter how dreary and gray our homes are, people would rather live there than in any other place. There is no place like home."

The Scarecrow sighed.

"Won't you tell me a story while we are resting?" Dorothy asked.

"My life has been so short that I really know nothing," said the Scarecrow. "I was only made the day before yesterday. Luckily, when the farmer made my head, one of the first things he did was to paint my ears, so that I heard what was going on.

"'Now I'll make the eyes,' said the farmer. So he painted my eyes. Then he made my nose and my mouth. I watched him make my body and my arms and legs. And when he fastened on my head, I felt very proud.

"'This fellow will scare the crows,' said the farmer. He carried me to the cornfield and set me up on a tall stick. Then he walked away.

"I tried to walk after him. But my feet would not touch the ground. It is a lonely life to be a scarecrow. By and by, an old crow flew near.

"'I wonder if that farmer thought to fool me,' said the crow. 'Any crow could see that you are stuffed with straw.' Then he hopped down at my feet and ate all the corn he wanted.

"I felt sad, for I was not such a good scarecrow

after all. But the old crow said,
'If you only had brains in your
head, you would be as good a man
as any of them.'

"After the crow had gone, I decided I
would try hard to get some brains. By good
luck, you came along. And from what you say,
I am sure the Great Oz will give me brains
as soon as we get to the Emerald City."

"I hope so," said Dorothy. "Let us go."

CHAPTER FOUR

# The Rescue of
# the Tin Woodman

Toward evening they came to a great forest. The trees grew big and close together.

"I see a little cottage," the Scarecrow said. "Shall we go there?"

"Yes, indeed," Dorothy answered.

So the Scarecrow led the way through the trees to the cottage. Inside, Dorothy found a bed of dried leaves. She lay down and, with Toto beside her, soon fell asleep.

When Dorothy awoke, the sun was shining. She sat up and looked around. There was the

Scarecrow, standing in a corner, waiting for her.

Dorothy, Toto, and the Scarecrow left the cottage and walked through the trees. Soon they found a spring of water. There, Dorothy drank and ate her breakfast. Suddenly, a groan came from nearby.

Dorothy and the Scarecrow turned. Dorothy gave a cry of surprise!

One of the big trees had been partly chopped through. Standing beside it was a man made entirely of tin. He held up an ax and stood perfectly still.

Toto barked and ran to snap at the tin legs.

"Did you groan?" asked Dorothy.

"Yes," answered the tin man. "I've been groaning for more than a year. No one has heard me before."

"What can I do for you?" asked Dorothy.

"Oil my joints," answered the tin man. "They

are rusted so badly that I cannot move. You will find an oilcan on a shelf in my cottage."

Dorothy ran back to the cottage. She found the oilcan and returned.

"Oil my neck first," said the Tin Woodman. So she oiled it.

"Now oil the joints in my arms," he said. Dorothy oiled them, too.

The Tin Woodman gave a sigh. He lowered his ax and leaned it against the tree. "That is a great comfort," he said. "I have been holding that ax up ever since I rusted. Now, if you will oil the joints of my legs, I shall be all right."

So Dorothy oiled his legs until the tin man could move freely. He thanked Dorothy and the Scarecrow. "You have saved my life. How did you happen to be here?"

"We are on our way to the Emerald City to see the Great Oz," answered Dorothy.

"Why do you wish to see Oz?" the Tin Woodman asked.

"I want him to send me back to Kansas. And the Scarecrow wants him to put brains into his head," Dorothy replied.

The Tin Woodman thought for a moment. "Do you suppose Oz could give me a heart?"

"Why, I guess so," Dorothy answered.

"Come along," said the Scarecrow.

So the Tin Woodman shouldered his ax. Dorothy, Toto, the Scarecrow, and the Tin Woodman walked through the forest.

When they came to the yellow brick road, the Scarecrow stumbled into a hole.

"Why didn't you walk around the hole?" asked the Tin Woodman.

"I don't know enough," replied the Scarecrow. "My head is stuffed with straw. That is why I am going to ask Oz for some brains."

"Oh, I see," said the Tin Woodman. "But brains are not the best things in the world. I would much rather have a heart."

"Why is that?" asked the Scarecrow.

While they walked, the Tin Woodman told his story.

"I was born the son of a woodman," said the tin man. "When I grew up, I, too, became a wood-chopper.

"There was a Munchkin girl I loved with all my heart. She promised to marry me as soon as I built a house for her. But the girl lived with an old woman who did not want her to marry, since the girl did her housework. So the old woman went to the Wicked Witch of the East, who enchanted my ax. When I was chopping wood one day, the ax slipped and cut off my leg.

"I went to a tinsmith and had him make me a new leg out of tin. The leg worked very well. But when I began chopping again, my ax slipped and cut off my other leg! Again I went to the tinsmith, who made me a leg out of tin. After this the enchanted ax cut off my arms. I had them replaced

with tin ones. The Wicked Witch then made the ax cut off my head. But the tinsmith even made me a new head of tin.

"I thought I had beaten the Wicked Witch. I worked harder than ever. But she made my ax slip again. This time it cut right through my body. The tinsmith made me a body of tin. But, alas! I had no heart. I lost all my love for the girl. I did not care whether I married her or not.

"Finally, there came a day when I was caught in a rainstorm, my joints rusted, and I was left to stand in the woods.

"It was terrible, but during the year I stood there, I had time to think. I decided that the greatest loss I had known was the loss of my heart. While I was in love, I was the happiest man on earth. But no one can love who doesn't have a heart. So I will ask Oz to give me one."

CHAPTER FIVE

# The Cowardly Lion

All this time Dorothy and her companions had been walking through the thick woods.

Suddenly, there came a terrible roar, and a great lion bounded into the road! With one blow of his paw, the Lion sent the Scarecrow spinning to the edge of the road.

Toto ran toward the Lion. The great beast opened his mouth to bite the dog.

Dorothy rushed forward. She slapped the Lion as hard as she could! "Don't you dare bite Toto!" she shouted. "You ought to be ashamed of yourself. A big beast like you, biting a poor little dog!"

"But I didn't bite him," said the Lion.

"No, but you tried to," Dorothy said. "You are nothing but a big coward!"

"I know," the Lion said. He hung his head in shame.

"To think of your striking a stuffed man like the Scarecrow!" said Dorothy.

"Is he stuffed?" asked the Lion in surprise. He watched Dorothy pick up the Scarecrow and set him upon his feet.

"Of course he's stuffed," replied Dorothy.

"What is that little animal?" asked the Lion.

"He is my dog, Toto," answered Dorothy.

"Oh! He seems remarkably small, now that I look at him. No one would think of biting such a little thing except a coward like me," said the Lion sadly.

"What makes you a coward?" asked Dorothy.

"I was born that way," replied the Lion.

"Whenever there is danger, my heart begins to beat fast."

"You ought to be glad, for that proves you *have* a heart," said the Tin Woodman.

"Perhaps," said the Lion.

"Have you brains?" asked the Scarecrow.

"I suppose so," said the Lion.

"I am going to the Great Oz to ask him to give me some," said the Scarecrow.

"And I am going to ask him to give me a heart," said the Woodman.

"And I am going to ask him to send Toto and me back to Kansas," said Dorothy.

"Then, if you don't mind, I'll go with you," said the Lion. "My life is unbearable without a bit of courage, and maybe the Great Oz can give me some."

"You will be very welcome," answered Dorothy,

"for you will help to keep away the other wild beasts."

So once more the little company set off. Only one thing of interest happened the rest of that day.

The Tin Woodman stepped on a beetle. He cried until tears ran down his face and rusted the hinges of his jaws. He made motions with his hands to Dorothy, trying to explain what had happened.

She did not understand. The Lion was also puzzled.

Finally, the Scarecrow seized the oilcan from Dorothy's basket. He oiled the Woodman's jaws. After a few moments the tin man could talk as well as before.

Thereafter the Tin Woodman walked very carefully, with his eyes on the road.

## CHAPTER SIX

# The Journey to the Great Oz

That night the companions camped out under a tree. When it was daylight, they started again toward the Emerald City.

They had been walking an hour when they came upon a great ditch. It was very wide and very deep, and it divided the forest as far as they could see. There were jagged rocks at the bottom. The sides were so steep that none of them could climb down.

"What shall we do?" asked Dorothy.

After serious thought the Scarecrow said,

"Here is a great tree. The Tin Woodman can chop it down. It will fall to the other side. That way we can walk across it."

So the Woodman set to work. Then the Lion put his front legs against the tree and pushed. Crash! The big tree fell across the ditch, just as the Scarecrow had suggested.

Just then a growl made them all look up. Two great beasts were running toward them! The beasts had bodies like bears and heads like tigers.

"Kalidahs!" said the Cowardly Lion. "I'm terribly afraid of them!"

"Quick!" cried the Scarecrow. "Let us cross over."

Dorothy went first, holding Toto. The Tin Woodman followed. The Scarecrow came next. Then the Lion turned to face the Kalidahs. He gave a loud roar.

The fierce beasts stopped short. But seeing

they were bigger than the Lion, the Kalidahs rushed forward. The Lion crossed over the tree. The Kalidahs came after him!

"They will tear us to pieces," the Lion said. "Stand close behind me, and I will fight."

"Wait a minute!" called the Scarecrow. He asked the Woodman to chop the end of the tree on their side of the ditch.

The Woodman did so. Just as the two Kalidahs were nearly across, the tree fell with a crash into the gulf. Both were dashed to pieces on the sharp rocks at the bottom.

This adventure made the travelers eager to get out of the forest. So they walked fast. In the afternoon they came upon a river.

"How shall we cross?" asked Dorothy.

"That is easily done," replied the Scarecrow. "The Tin Woodman must build us a raft."

When night fell, the raft was not finished. So

they found a cozy place under the trees to sleep. Dorothy dreamed of the Emerald City and of the Great Wizard, Oz, who would soon send her back to her own home again.

The travelers awakened the next morning refreshed and full of hope. The Tin Woodman finished the raft, and they were ready to start. They had long poles to push the raft through the water.

They got along quite well until they reached the middle of the river. There the current turned swift. It swept the raft downstream. They went farther and farther away from the yellow brick road.

"We must get to the Emerald City," the Scarecrow said.

He pushed so hard on his pole that it stuck in the mud at the bottom of the river. Before he could pull it out, the raft was swept away! The

Scarecrow was left clinging to the pole in the middle of the river.

Down the stream the raft floated. The poor Scarecrow was far behind.

"Something must be done!" said the Lion.

He sprang into the water. The Tin Woodman stayed on the raft and caught hold of his tail. Then the Lion swam with all his might. It was hard work, but by and by, they were drawn out of the current.

Dorothy took the Tin Woodman's long pole and helped push the raft to the land. The stream had carried them a long way past the yellow brick road.

"We must find the Scarecrow," said the Tin Woodman.

They started along the grassy bank.

After a time Dorothy cried out, "Look!"

There was the Scarecrow, perched upon his pole in the middle of the water!

A stork landed at the water's edge. "Who are you?" asked the stork.

"I am Dorothy," Dorothy answered. "These are my friends. But we have to rescue the Scarecrow. Can you help?"

So the big bird flew to the Scarecrow. She picked him up by the arm and carried him to the bank.

The Scarecrow hugged his three friends. "I was afraid I would have to stay in the river forever!"

They thanked the stork and walked along. Soon they found themselves in a great meadow of poppies.

Now, it is well known that when there are many of these flowers, anyone who breathes their

odor will fall asleep. And a sleeper who is not carried away from the flowers can sleep forever. Dorothy did not know this. Her eyes grew heavy. Soon she fell among the poppies, fast asleep.

"What shall we do?" asked the Tin Woodman.

"If we leave her here, she will die," said the Lion. "And I can scarcely keep my eyes open. Look, the dog is asleep, too."

It was true. Toto had fallen down beside Dorothy. Luckily, the Scarecrow and the Tin Woodman were not made of flesh, so they were untroubled by the flowers.

"Run," said the Scarecrow to the Lion. "Get out of this flower bed. We will carry Dorothy and Toto."

The Lion bounded away as fast as he could go. Then the Scarecrow and the Tin Woodman put Toto in Dorothy's lap. They carried the sleeping girl through the flowers.

in a pretty spot be-

poppies. Then they

waken her.

## CHAPTER SEVEN

# The Guardian of the Gates

When Dorothy and Toto awakened, the companions started on their journey once again. It was not long before they reached the yellow brick road and turned toward the Emerald City.

The road was smooth and well paved. They soon saw a beautiful green glow in the sky.

"That must be the Emerald City," Dorothy said.

In the afternoon, they came to the great green wall around the City. At the end of the yellow brick road was a big gate, studded with emeralds.

ound themselves in

walls glistened with

em. He was clothed

was greenish. At his

Emerald City?" the

reat Oz," answered

ace anyone asked to

he Guardian of the

ee the Great Oz, I

t first you must put

e brightness of the

u," said the Guardian of the Gates. "Even those who live in the City must wear spectacles night and day."

The Guardian of the Gates opened the large green box. It was filled with spectacles! Each pair had lenses of green glass. The Guardian found a pair for Dorothy. Then he fitted spectacles for the Scarecrow, the Tin Woodman, the Lion, and even little Toto. Finally, the Guardian of the Gates put on his own glasses. He opened another gate.

The friends followed him into the Emerald City. Even with the green spectacles, Dorothy and her companions were dazzled. The houses were built of green marble. They were studded with emeralds. Even the sky had a green tint!

The Guardian of the Gates led them through the streets to the Palace of Oz. There was a soldier before the door. He was dressed in green, too, and had a long green beard.

"Here are strangers," said the Guardian of the Gates to him. "They demand to see the Great Oz."

"Step inside," said the soldier. "I will carry your message to him."

When the soldier came back, Dorothy asked, "Have you seen Oz yourself?"

"Oh, no," returned the soldier. "I have never seen him. But he sat behind his screen and I gave him your message. He said he would grant you an audience. But each one of you must see him alone. I will have you shown to rooms where you may wait in comfort."

"Thank you," Dorothy said. "That is very kind."

The soldier blew a green whistle. A girl entered the room. She had lovely green hair and green eyes.

"I will show you to your rooms," the girl said.

## CHAPTER EIGHT

# The Wonderful
# City of Oz

The next morning, after breakfast, the green maiden came to fetch Dorothy. They started for the Throne Room of the Palace. The girl opened a door and Dorothy walked through.

She found herself in a big, round room. The walls and ceiling and floor were covered with emeralds. A green marble throne stood in the middle, and in the chair was an enormous Head!

The mouth moved and a voice said, "I am Oz, the Great and Terrible. Who are you, and why do you seek me?"

It was not as awful a voice as Dorothy had expected. So she took courage.

"I am Dorothy," she said. "I have come to you for help."

The eyes looked at her. "Where did you get the silver shoes?"

"I got them from the Wicked Witch of the East, when my house fell on her and killed her," Dorothy replied.

"Where did you get the mark upon your forehead?" asked Oz.

"That is where the Good Witch of the North kissed me," said the girl.

"What do you wish me to do?" Oz asked.

"Send me back to Kansas," said Dorothy. "Aunt Em will be dreadfully worried over my being away so long."

"Well," said Oz, "if you wish me to use my magic power, you must do something for me first."

"What must I do?" asked Dorothy.

"Kill the Wicked Witch of the West," answered Oz.

Dorothy began to weep. "Even if I wanted to, how could I kill the Wicked Witch?"

"I do not know," said the Head. "But that is my answer. Now go. And do not ask to see me again until you have done your task."

Dorothy left the Throne Room. She went back to where the Lion and the Scarecrow and the Tin Woodman were waiting for her. "There is no hope for me," she said sadly.

The next day the soldier with the green beard came for the Scarecrow. The Scarecrow followed him into the Throne Room. On the emerald throne was a lovely Lady.

"I am Oz, the Great and Terrible," the lady said sweetly. "Who are you, and why do you seek me?"

The Scarecrow was surprised. He had expected to see the giant Head that Dorothy had told him about.

"I am only a scarecrow stuffed with straw," he said bravely. "I come to ask you to put brains in my head."

"Why should I do this for you?" asked the Lady.

"Because you are wise and powerful," answered the Scarecrow.

"I never grant favors without something in return," said the Lady. "But if you kill the Wicked Witch of the West, I will give you a great many brains."

"I thought you asked Dorothy to kill the Witch," said the Scarecrow.

"So I did," said the Lady. "I don't care who kills her. But until she is dead, I will not grant your wish."

The Scarecrow went back to his friends and told them what Oz had said.

The next morning the soldier with the green beard came for the Tin Woodman. When the Woodman entered the great Throne Room, he saw that Oz had taken the shape of a most terrible Beast.

"I am Oz, the Great and Terrible," roared the Beast. "Who are you, and why do you seek me?"

"I am a woodman, made of tin. I pray you to give me a heart," said the Tin Woodman.

Oz gave a low growl. "Help Dorothy kill the Wicked Witch of the West and I will give you the biggest, most loving heart in all the Land of Oz."

The Tin Woodman returned to

his friends. He told them what Oz had said to him.

The next day was the Lion's turn. On the throne was a Ball of Fire.

A low, quiet voice came from the Ball of Fire. "I am Oz, the Great and Terrible. Who are you, and why do you seek me?"

The Lion answered, "I am a cowardly lion, and I beg that you give me courage."

The Ball of Fire burned fiercely. "Bring me proof that the Wicked Witch is dead. At that moment I will give you courage. Until then, you must remain a coward."

The Lion was angry but said nothing.

He was glad to find his friends waiting for him, and told them of his terrible interview with the Wizard.

"What shall we do?" asked Dorothy sadly.

"There is only one thing we *can* do," said the Lion. "We must seek out the Wicked Witch and destroy her!"

## CHAPTER NINE

# The Wicked Witch
## of the West

The following day the soldier with the green beard came for Dorothy, the Scarecrow, the Tin Woodman, and the Cowardly Lion. He led them through the Emerald City to where the Guardian of the Gates lived.

"Which road leads to the Wicked Witch of the West?" Dorothy asked.

"There is no road," answered the Guardian of the Gates. "No one ever wishes to go that way."

"How, then, are we to find her?" Dorothy asked.

"Keep to the West, where the sun sets, and you cannot fail to find her," the Guardian replied.

The travelers followed his advice, and the Emerald City was soon far behind them.

Now, the Wicked Witch of the West had only one eye. But that eye was as powerful as a telescope, and it could see everywhere. So it happened that she saw Dorothy and her friends coming her way.

The Wicked Witch stamped her foot and tore her hair when she saw the intruders. She took a charmed Golden Cap from her cupboard. Whoever wore the Cap could call upon an army of Winged Monkeys.

So the Wicked Witch placed

ad. Then she said

e was a rushing of
Monkeys gathered
ach Monkey had a

" the biggest Mon-

are within my land
Wicked Witch. "Ex-
ne."

e obeyed," said the

When they reached Dorothy and her friends, some of the Monkeys seized the Tin Woodman. They carried him to a place with sharp rocks and dropped him there. The Tin Woodman lay battered and dented.

Other Monkeys pulled all of the straw out of the Scarecrow. They bundled his hat and boots and clothes together and threw them into a tall tree.

The remaining Monkeys threw rope around the Lion and carried him to the Witch's Castle. They put him in a yard with a high iron fence.

Dorothy waited with Toto in her arms.

The leader of the Winged Monkeys flew up to her, meaning harm. But when he saw the mark of the Good Witch's kiss on her forehead, he said, "We dare not harm this little girl. The Power of Good protects her, and that is greater than the Power of Evil. All we can do is to take her to the

Castle of the Wicked Witch."

So Dorothy and Toto were carried to the Castle's doorstep.

The Monkey leader said to the Witch, "We have obeyed you as far as we were able. Your power over our band is now ended."

Then all the Winged Monkeys took to the air and were soon out of sight.

## CHAPTER TEN

# The Rescue

The Wicked Witch saw the mark on Dorothy's forehead and the silver shoes. She trembled with fear, for she knew they had a powerful charm in them. Then the Witch realized that Dorothy did not know how to use the power she had.

"Come with me," the Wicked Witch of the West said to Dorothy.

Dorothy followed the Witch to the Castle kitchen. The Wicked Witch ordered her to clean the pots and kettles and sweep the floor.

It so happened that the Wicked Witch wanted the silver shoes for herself. But Dorothy never took them off except to sleep and when she took her bath.

The Witch was too afraid of the dark to go in Dorothy's room at night, and her fear of water was greater than her fear of the dark. Indeed, the old Witch never let water touch her in any way.

Days and nights passed. Finally, the Witch thought of a trick that would give her what she wanted. She placed an iron bar in the middle of the kitchen floor. Then she made the iron invisible.

Dorothy walked across the floor and stumbled over the bar. She was not hurt, but one of the silver shoes came off. The Witch snatched it up.

In a fit of anger, Dorothy picked up a bucket of water and threw it over the Witch.

The Witch gave a cry, and then she began to shrink!

"See what you have done!" she screamed. "In a minute I shall melt away."

"I'm very sorry," said Dorothy, which perhaps she was.

"Didn't you know water would be the end of me?" wailed the Witch. "Soon I shall be all melted and you will have the Castle to yourself! Look out—here I go!"

With these words the Witch became a brown shapeless mass. Dorothy filled another bucket with water and threw it over the mess. Then she swept it all out the door.

Dorothy picked up her silver shoe, cleaned it, and put it on her foot again. Then she ran to tell the Lion that they were no longer prisoners.

Not only was the Cowardly Lion happy about the melting of the Wicked Witch, but so were the Winkies. The Winkies were the people who lived in the Land of the West. The Wicked Witch had never been nice to them.

"If the Scarecrow and the Tin Woodman were

with us, I would be quite happy," the Lion told Dorothy.

"Do you suppose we could rescue them?" asked Dorothy.

"We can try," answered the Lion.

The Winkies were delighted to help Dorothy in any way they could. They traveled all over their land until they found the battered Tin Woodman. They carried him back to the castle.

There, Winkie tinsmiths worked for three days and four nights. They hammered and twisted and pounded and polished. Finally, the tin man was all fixed!

The Tin Woodman was so pleased that he wept tears of joy. Dorothy had to wipe every tear with her apron so his joints would not be rusted.

"If we only had the Scarecrow with us," said the Tin Woodman, "I would be quite happy."

The Winkies searched all over the land until

they found the Scarecrow's clothes in a tall tree.

"I'll chop the tree down," said the Tin Wood-man when the Winkies told him.

In a short time the tree fell. Dorothy picked up the Scarecrow's clothes. The Winkies carried them back to the Castle. They stuffed the clothes with nice, clean straw. And behold! The Scarecrow was as good as ever!

"And now we must go back to Oz and get our rewards," said Dorothy.

Dorothy went to the Witch's cupboard to fill her basket with food for the journey. There she saw the Golden Cap. She tried it on and it fitted her exactly. So she made up her mind to wear it.

Dorothy and her friends said good-bye to the Winkies, and they all started for the Emerald City. The Winkies gave them three cheers and many good wishes.

## CHAPTER ELEVEN

# The Winged Monkeys

You may remember that there was no road be-
tween the Castle of the Wicked Witch and the
Emerald City. The Winged Monkeys had brought
Dorothy and the Lion to the Castle.

"We have surely lost our way," the Scarecrow
said after they had been walking for a while.

Dorothy looked inside the Golden Cap. There
she saw some words on the Cap's lining. Now she
knew what to do. Dorothy put the Cap back on.
She said the same words that the Wicked Witch
had used:

*"Ep-pe, pep-pe, kak-ke!*
*Hil-lo, hol-lo, hel-lo!*
*Ziz-zy, zuz-zy, zik!"*

The sound of wings filled the air, and the band of Winged Monkeys landed before them.

The leader bowed low to Dorothy. "What is your command?" he asked.

"We wish to go to the Emerald City," said Dorothy.

No sooner had she spoken than two of the Monkeys caught her in their arms. More Monkeys carried the Scarecrow and the Woodman and the Lion. One little Monkey picked up Toto and flew after them.

In no time, Dorothy looked down and saw the shining green walls of the Emerald City. The Monkeys set the travelers down carefully before

the gate, and flew off as fast as they had appeared.

Dorothy, the Scarecrow, the Tin Woodman, and the Lion walked up and rang the bell. The Guardian of the Gates opened the gate. As before, he gave them spectacles before taking them through the gate and on to the Palace of Oz.

The soldier with the green beard was still there. He had the news of their return carried straight to Oz, but Oz made no reply. There was no word from him the next day, or the next.

At last, the Scarecrow asked the soldier to take another message to Oz. It said that if he did not see them, they would call on the Winged Monkeys to help them.

The Wizard sent word for them to come to the Throne Room the very next morning.

After they arrived at the Throne Room, Dorothy and her friends were surprised when they saw no one. Presently they heard a Voice. It seemed

ıg.

ıy do you

ise," said

d?" asked

ıer with a

sudden!

## CHAPTER TWELVE

# The Discovery of Oz the Terrible

Behind the fallen screen was a little old man with a bald head and a wrinkled face. He looked as surprised as they were.

"Who are you?" the Tin Woodman cried.

"I am Oz, the Great and Terrible," said the little man in a trembling voice.

"Aren't you a Great Wizard?" asked Dorothy.

"Hush," said the little man. "Don't speak so loud or you will be overheard. I'm *supposed* to be a Great Wizard."

Dorothy asked

lly. "I'm just a

he Scarecrow.

man. "I am a

t understand.
d?"

answered Oz.

in the back of

lay the great

and the mask

vely Lady that

man's terrible

sewn together.

ball of cotton

and lit with a

ou ought to be

ered the little

could do. Sit

ile he told the

na—" the little

"Why, that isn't very far from Kansas!" Dorothy exclaimed.

"When I grew up, I became a ventriloquist," Oz went on. "After a time, I tired of that. I became a balloonist.

"One day I went up in a balloon and the ropes got twisted. I couldn't come down. The balloon went way up above the clouds. For a day and a night, I traveled through the air. When I awoke, the balloon was floating over a strange and beautiful country.

"The balloon came down, and the people here thought I was a great wizard and wanted me to be their leader.

"I had them build this city. Then I thought that as the country is so green, I would call it the Emerald City. To make the name fit even better, I had everyone wear green spectacles, so that everything they see is green."

"But *isn't* everything here green?" asked Dorothy.

"No more than in any other city," replied Oz. "But when you wear green spectacles, of course everything looks green!

"I have been good to the people, and they like me. One of my only fears has been the Witches. The Witches of the North and South are good, but the Witches of the East and West were terribly wicked. So you can imagine how pleased I was when I heard your house had fallen on the Wicked Witch of the East.

"When you came to me, Dorothy, I was willing to promise anything if you would only do away with the other Wicked Witch. And you succeeded! However, I am ashamed to say that I cannot keep my promises."

## CHAPTER THIRTEEN

# The Truth

Dorothy and her friends looked at the little man in shock.

"Can't you give me brains?" asked the Scarecrow.

"Truthfully, you don't need brains," Oz told him. "You are learning something every day."

"That may be true," said the Scarecrow. "But I shall be very unhappy unless you give me brains."

The false Wizard looked at him. "Well," he said with a sigh, "I'm not much of a magician. But if you will come to me tomorrow morning, I will stuff your head with brains."

u!" cried the Scare-

" asked the Lion.

age," answered Oz.

There is no living

t faces danger. True

you are afraid, and

in plenty."

just the same," said

ppy unless you give

akes one forget he is

"And now," said Dorothy, "how am I to get back to Kansas?"

"We shall have to think about that," replied the little man. "Give me two or three days to consider the matter. I'll try to find a way to carry you over the desert. There is only one thing I ask in return. You must keep my secret."

They all agreed and went back to their rooms in high spirits. Even Dorothy had hope that the humbug would find a way to send her back to Kansas. If he did, she was willing to forgive him everything.

Next morning the Scarecrow went to the Throne Room and rapped upon the door.

"Come in," called Oz.

"I have come for my brains," said the Scarecrow.

"Sit down in that chair," Oz told him. The Wizard unfastened the Scarecrow's head. He emptied out the straw. He went into a back room and made a mixture of bran and pins and needles.

The Wizard filled the top of the Scarecrow's head with the mixture. Then he stuffed the rest of the space with straw to hold it in place.

When he replaced the Scarecrow's head on his body, the Scarecrow was pleased. He thanked Oz and went back to his friends.

Dorothy looked at the Scarecrow curiously. "How do you feel?" she asked.

"I feel wise, indeed," he answered.

"Now I will go and get my heart," said the Woodman.

In the Throne Room, Oz cut a small square in the left side of the Tin Woodman's chest. Then he fetched a red silk heart stuffed with sawdust. Oz put the heart in the Woodman's chest and replaced the square of tin. He soldered it together.

"There," said Oz. "Now you have a heart that any man might be proud of."

"I am very grateful!" exclaimed the Woodman, and went back to his friends.

Now the Lion went to the Throne Room for courage.

Oz went to a cupboard and took down a green bottle. He gave it to the Cowardly Lion and bade him drink.

ottle was empty.

Oz.

the Lion. He went

p being a humbug,"

eople make me do

:an't be done? But it

on to carry Dorothy

## CHAPTER FOURTEEN

# How the Balloon
# Was Launched

Dorothy waited for three days.

On the fourth day, Oz sent for her. When she went into the Throne Room, he said, "I think I have found the way to get you out of this country."

"How?" asked Dorothy.

"A balloon," said Oz. "We will fill it with hot air to make it carry us."

"Us!" exclaimed Dorothy. "Are you going with me?"

"Yes, of course," replied Oz. "I am tired of

being a humbug. I'd much rather go back to Kansas. If you will help me sew the silk together, we will begin to work on our balloon."

Oz cut strips of silk and Dorothy sewed them together. When it was all finished, they had a big bag of green silk: a balloon!

Oz sent the soldier with the green beard for a big clothes basket. He fastened it to the bottom of the balloon.

Soldiers carried the balloon to the front of the Palace. The people looked at it with curiosity. The Tin Woodman chopped a big pile of wood at the front of the Palace as well. Now the wood was lit.

The balloon was held over the fire. Hot air filled the silk bag. The balloon swelled. It rose until the basket just touched the ground.

Then Oz climbed into the basket.

"I am going away for a visit," he said to all the people. "While I am gone, the Scarecrow will rule over you."

The balloon tugged at the ropes that held it to the ground.

"Come, Dorothy!" cried the Wizard. "Hurry up, or the balloon will fly away."

But Toto had run into the crowd after a kitten, and Dorothy had run after him! At last, she scooped up the little dog and ran toward the balloon. She was only a few steps away when—crack! The ropes broke.

The balloon rose into the air.

"Come back!" Dorothy screamed. "I want to go, too!"

"I can't come back," called Oz from the basket. "Good-bye!"

to us. We can do as

e," said Dorothy. "I

nd Uncle Henry in

done?" asked the

n the green beard,"

ned.

"This little girl," said the Scarecrow, "wishes to cross the desert."

"Is there no one who can help me?" asked Dorothy.

"Glinda can help you," the soldier said. "She is the Witch of the South, the most powerful of all the Witches. Her Castle stands on the edge of the desert."

"How can I get to her Castle?" asked Dorothy.

"The road is straight to the south," he answered. "Glinda lives in the Land of the Quadlings."

"I shall go with Dorothy," declared the Lion.

"So shall I," said the Tin Woodman.

"When do we start?" asked the Scarecrow.

"You are all very kind," said Dorothy. "I would like to go as soon as possible!"

"This little girl," Scarecrow, "wishes to cross the desert"

Is there anyone who can help her asked Dorothy

"Glinda can help you," the soldier said. "She is the Witch of the South, the most powerful of all the Witches. Her Castle stands on the edge of the

## CHAPTER FIFTEEN·

# Away to the South

The sun shone brightly the next day. The four companions turned their faces toward the Land of the South. They were in the best of spirits. Dorothy was once more filled with the hope of getting home.

The first day's journey was through the green fields that stretched about the Emerald City. They slept that night on the grass with the stars over them.

In the morning they traveled on. Soon they came to a thick wood that was so huge, there was no way of going around it. They looked for a place to enter the forest.

Finally, the Scarecrow discovered a big tree with such wide branches that they could pass underneath. But when he walked under the tree, the branches bent down, lifted him up, and threw him back to the others!

This did not hurt him. But he was rather dizzy when Dorothy picked him up. The Scarecrow went to another tree. The same thing happened!

"How strange!" said Dorothy.

"The trees don't want to let us pass," said the Lion.

"I will try it myself," said the Woodman. He marched up to the first tree. A big branch bent down, and the Woodman cut it in two.

"Come on!" he shouted to the others. "Be quick!"

They all ran under the tree into the woods! It seemed that only the first row of trees could bend their branches—as if they were the policemen of the forest.

Dorothy, Toto, the Scarecrow, the Tin Woodman, and the Cowardly Lion walked on until they came to the other side of the wood. To their surprise, they found a high wall.

They climbed up and jumped down on the other side.

The country before them was as smooth as a platter. Scattered around were houses made of china. There were also china barns with china fences. And there were cows and sheep and pigs and chickens. They were all made of china. The people were china, too.

"We must be very careful here," said the Tin Woodman, "or we may hurt these pretty little people."

They walked carefully through the china country. After an hour or so they came to another wall. They scrambled over it and found themselves in a wild forest. They walked through it until they arrived in the country of the Quadlings.

## CHAPTER SIXTEEN

# The Good Witch Grants Dorothy's Wish

The Land of the Quadlings was rich and happy. There were fields of ripening grain. Everything— fences and houses and bridges—was painted bright red. The Quadlings themselves were dressed all in red.

Dorothy and her friends walked by the fields and across the red bridges. Soon they came to a beautiful Castle. Before the gates were three girls dressed in red uniforms. As Dorothy and her friends drew near, one of the girls asked, "Why have you come to the South Country?"

who rules here,"

ke me to her?"

a big room.

upon a throne of

ringlets over her

y child?" she asked.

story, ending with,

ck to Kansas. Aunt

dful has happened

our silver shoes will

ou had known their

home the day you

"And I would have lived a coward forever," declared the Lion.

"This is all true," said Dorothy. "And I am glad that I helped you all. But now I would like to go back to Kansas, where I belong."

"All you have to do is to tap your heels together three times and command the shoes to carry you wherever you wish to go," said Glinda.

Dorothy threw her arms around the Lion's neck. She kissed him. Then she kissed the Tin Woodman. Then she hugged the soft, stuffed body of the Scarecrow.

Glinda the Good Witch stepped down from her ruby throne. She gave Dorothy a good-bye kiss.

Dorothy took Toto up in her arms. Then she tapped the heels of her shoes together three times. "Take me home to Aunt Em!" she said.

Instantly she was whirling through the air. Then she stopped so suddenly that she rolled over in the grass several times. She sat up and looked about.

"Good gracious!" Dorothy cried. For she was sitting on the Kansas prairie. Before her was a new farmhouse, one that Uncle Henry had built after the cyclone had carried away the old one.

Aunt Em came out the front door. She looked up and saw Dorothy running toward her. "My

darling child!" she cried. She folded the little girl in her arms. "Where in the world did you come from?"

"From the Land of Oz," said Dorothy. "And here is Toto, too. And oh, Aunt Em! I'm so glad to be home!"

## About the Author

L. FRANK BAUM was born on May 15, 1856, in Chittenango, New York. He grew up on a country estate called Rose Lawn, his father having made a fortune. As an adult, Baum worked in the theater, newspapers, and magazines, manufactured axle grease, managed a general store, and raised chickens! In 1900, *The Wonderful Wizard of Oz* was published and became an overnight success. Two years later, a musical version of the book was produced onstage, with Baum writing the lyrics. He wrote fourteen Oz books and nine other fantasies. More authors contributed to the Oz series, making a total of forty books. The famous movie starring Judy Garland came out in 1939, twenty years after Baum's death in 1919.

# About the Illustrator

W. W. DENSLOW was born in Philadelphia on May 5, 1856. By the time he turned twenty, he was working for magazines and newspapers all over the country. In the 1890s, he moved to Chicago, where he met L. Frank Baum. They worked on several books together, including *The Wonderful Wizard of Oz,* but they had a disagreement over the profits from the stage musical. As a result, *The Wonderful Wizard of Oz* is the only Oz book that Denslow illustrated. He went on to become one

 of the best-known and most prolific American artists of the turn of the century. He died in 1915.

STEPPING STONES
a chapter book

CLASSIC

ALICE in WONDERLAND

by Lewis Carroll
adapted by Mallory Loehr

What would you do if a white rabbit
with a pocket watch ran by you
on a lazy summer day? Alice follows it,
down a rabbit hole to Wonderland!

What would you do if a white rabbit
with a pocket watch ran by you
on a lazy summer day? Alice follows it
down a rabbit hole to Wonderland!